Not a Pot

Written by Leilani Sparrow
Illustrated by Rosie Brooks

Collins

It is a map.

Tick the pad, Kim.

3

Nick packs a cap.

Pack the kit, Kim.

Kim digs a pit.

Kim can dig it.

It is a pot.

Nick sits and sips.

Can Nick dig a pot?

Kim sits and sips.

Nick digs and digs.

It is not a pot.

/c/

14

/k/ /ck/

After reading

Letters and Sounds: Phase 2

Word count: 50

Focus phonemes: /g/ /o/ /c/ /k/ ck

Common exception words: a, is, the

Curriculum links: Understanding the World: The World

Early learning goals: Listening and attention: Listen to stories, accurately anticipating key events and respond to what is heard with relevant comments, questions or actions; Understanding: answer 'how' and 'why' questions about experiences and in response to stories or events; Reading: children use phonic knowledge to decode regular words and read them aloud accurately; they also read some common irregular words.

Developing fluency

- Go back and read the chant to your child, using lots of expression.
- Make sure that your child follows as you read.
- Pause so they can join in and read with you.
- Say the whole chant together. You can make up some actions to go with the words.

It is a map.	Kim digs a pit.	Can Nick dig a pot?
Tick the pad, Kim.	Kim can do it.	Kim sits and sips.
Nick packs a cap.	It is a pot.	Nick digs and digs.
Pack the kit, Kim	Nick sits and sips.	It is not a pot.

Phonic practice

- Point to the word **Kim** on page 5. Model sounding it out 'K-i-m' and blending the sounds together **Kim**. Explain that it is a name and so it starts with a capital letter. Ask your child if they can find another word on page 5 that begins with the sound /k/. (*kit*) Ask them to sound out the word and then blend the sounds together.
- Now look at the I spy sounds pages (14–15) together. Which words can your child find in the picture with the /k/, /c/ or /ck/ sounds in them? (e.g. *koala, crocodile, kangaroo, kite, cake, kitten, carrot, bucket*)